It's Not FUnny!

www.**booksattransworld**.co.uk/childrens

Also available by Jan Page
and published by Corgi Pups:

DOG ON A BROOMSTICK
DOGNAPPED!
THE CHOCOLATE MONSTER

It's Not FUnny!

Jan Page

Illustrated by Tony Ross

For Harry

IT'S NOT FUNNY!
A CORGI PUP BOOK: 0 552 546577

First publication in Great Britain

PRINTING HISTORY
Corgi Pups edition published 2001

1 3 5 7 9 10 8 6 4 2

Set in 18/25 pt Bembo MT Schoolbook by Falcon Oast Graphic Art

Corgi Books are published by Transworld Publishers,
61–63 Uxbridge Road, London W5 5SA,
a division of The Random House Group Ltd,
in Australia by Random House Australia (Pty) Ltd,
20 Alfred Street, Milsons Point, Sydney, NSW 2061, Australia,
in New Zealand by Random House New Zealand Ltd,
18 Poland Road, Glenfield, Auckland 10, New Zealand
and in South Africa by Random House (Pty) Ltd,
Endulini, 5A Jubilee Road, Parktown 2193, South Africa

Made and printed in Great Britain by
Cox & Wyman Ltd, Reading, Berkshire

Contents

Series Reading Consultant: Prue Goodwin,
Reading and Language Information Centre,
University of Reading

Chapter One

Bill was a clown. He called himself *The Great Bilbo* and he wanted to work in the circus.

The Great Bilbo could pull silly
faces and speak in funny voices.
He could balance a spoon on
the end of his nose whilst eating
spaghetti.

He was fantastic at falling over
and knew forty-seven jokes by
heart.

Every morning the Great Bilbo
somersaulted out of bed and
dressed in a pair of baggy
trousers, a yellow shirt, a silly
blue wig and a red plastic nose.

And every morning, Mum made
him take it all off and put on his
school uniform.

"What's green and yellow and hops?" croaked the Great Bilbo, leaping round the bedroom as he pulled on his trousers.

"A frog with custard on his head," answered Mum, who'd heard all Bill's jokes before. "Now, what do you want for breakfast?"

Bill did funny walks and told
jokes all the way to school.

Mum told him off for dawdling
and he was the last to line up in
the playground.

The Great Bilbo clowned
about so much that he had to
move to the table nearest the
teacher's desk. He thought it
was so that Miss Carter could
listen to his jokes, but she never
laughed at any of them.

He was sad when she took away his red pencil-pot, because it made a rather good clown nose. Although the blue pencil-pot turned out to have its advantages – he could pretend he was a clown standing in the cold.

When Miss Carter called Bill's name in the register he replied, "Yes, Miss Carpet!" The day before he had said "Yes, Miss Carrot," and the day before that he had called her Miss Caravan. Everyone burst out laughing – everyone, that is, except the teacher.

"It's not funny!" insisted Miss Carter. And she made him stay in at break to wash the paint-pots.

At lunch-time, the Great
Bilbo took three satsumas and
performed a juggling show for
Reception Table. They all had
giggling fits and two of them
knocked their drinks over.

Then a satsuma landed in a dollop of mashed potato and splattered a little girl in the face.

This gave the Great Bilbo a wonderful idea. He would show them how to throw a custard pie!

He made his mashed potato
into a large, lumpy ball, stood
on his chair and launched it
across the room – *wheee!* – just
as Mrs Mitchell, the Head
Dinner Lady, was coming to see
what all the noise was about.

Splat! The 'custard pie' hit her full in the face. Everyone in the dinner hall fell about laughing, but Mrs Mitchell was furious.

She sent the Great Bilbo to
stand outside the Headmistress's
office and he had to miss all his
lunch-time play.

Bill didn't mind too much. It
gave him the chance to practise
his silly faces. Then the
Headmistress walked by and
saw him sticking his tongue out.

"I was only seeing if my tongue would touch my nose," explained Bill. But the Headmistress didn't seem to believe him.

"Tell your mother to come and see me after school," she said. "I want to have a little word."

The Great Bilbo tried to imagine what that 'little word' might be. "Pig" perhaps, or "moo" . . .? His thoughts made him want to giggle, and the corners of his mouth started twitching.

But the Headmistress was not in
the mood for any more of the
Great Bilbo's humour.

"We've all had enough of
your clowning about," she said.
"Can't you understand? It's
NOT funny!"

Bill waited for ages while Mum spoke to the Headmistress. He calculated they must have had hundreds of words of all sizes. When she finally came out of the office, Mum's face was bright red.

"How can the teacher teach
if you're constantly mucking
about? It's got to stop!"

"But I'm the Great Bilbo," said
Bill, balancing on the playground
wall as if it were a tightrope.

"This is serious, Bill. Any
more bad behaviour and I won't
take you to the circus on
Saturday." Bill looked at her in
horror. He had been looking
forward to the circus for weeks!

So for the next three days, the
Great Bilbo did his clowning in
secret. He locked
himself in the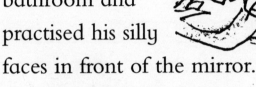
bathroom and
practised his silly
faces in front of the mirror.

 He learnt
another five jokes
from his *One
Hundred Best Jokes
Book* – but he
only tried them out on the dog.
And on Friday afternoon, the
Great Bilbo was told he could
go to the circus after all! Phew!

Chapter Two

The next morning the Great
Bilbo leapt out of bed at five
o'clock and dressed in his baggy
trousers, yellow shirt, silly blue
wig and red plastic nose. He
covered his face in white make-
up and painted on a big red grin.

The time seemed to pass ever so slowly! The Great Bilbo was so excited he could only manage half a marmite sandwich for lunch. But at last, half-past one arrived, and they caught the bus to the circus.

The Big Top was in a park on the outskirts of town. It was enormous! By the time they had found their seats, the music was already playing and coloured lights were darting across the circus ring.

Bill enjoyed the trapeze
artists, but he thought the
dancing horses were boring. He
liked the sparkly acrobats who
jumped off see-saws and he

thought the lady who balanced
a sword on the end of
her nose was very
clever (he promised
Mum he wouldn't try
it at home).
In the interval
he drank a
cup of warm
Coke and
managed three
mouthfuls
of candy-
floss. Then
it was the
clowns!

There were six of them, all different shapes and sizes. They rode into the circus ring on a tiny fire engine, ringing bells and sounding hooters. Bill cheered as loudly as he could and clapped until his palms felt sore.

The boss clown wore a tall white hat and a strange costume that was almost a dress. He had white tights and black ballet shoes on his feet. His face was white too and he spoke to the audience using a microphone on a very long lead.

"Ladeez and gentlemen, my name is Frederico! We need a new clown to join our show! Does any leetle boy or girl want to be a clown?"

"Me! Me!" cried the Great Bilbo. About two hundred other children had the same idea. The clown scanned the crowd.

"Ze leetle girl in ze pink dress!" he shouted, holding out his hand. The girl giggled and stepped daintily into the circus ring. Bill couldn't understand it.

"It's not fair!" he cried. "She doesn't look anything like a clown!"

"OK, leetle girl clown, first I teach you how to juggle!" said Frederico. He took out three juggling balls and told her to throw them up in the air.

The balls went everywhere, and one hit Frederico on the bottom.

He jumped about the ring, pretending she had hurt him, while everyone laughed.

"She's hopeless!" moaned the Great Bilbo, tearfully. "Why didn't they choose me?"

"Never mind," said Mum. "I'll buy us some popcorn." She left her seat and joined a very long queue at the back of the circus tent.

Bill watched in dismay as the little girl tried to throw custard pies at the clowns' faces. She was giggling so much that she kept missing. The audience seemed to find it very amusing, but the Great Bilbo could bear it no longer. He clambered over the seats and jumped into the ring!

Chapter Three

"And who might you be?" asked Frederico, looking very surprised.

"The Great Bilbo!" declared Bill, bowing. He took out his juggling balls and began to perform. The crowd clapped and cheered.

"What did the earwig say when he got to the edge of the cliff?" shouted the Great Bilbo. "Earwigo!"

The audience groaned, then burst out laughing.

Next, Bill took a plastic banana-skin from his pocket and threw it onto the ground.

Then he pretended to slip and
did a spectacular piece of falling
over. He got such a huge round
of applause, that he did it all
over again.

"Very good, leetle clown!
Zank you very much!" boomed
the clown. Then he bent
down and whispered
in Bill's ear. "Now go
back to your seat, OK?"

"But I haven't done my show yet!" insisted Bill. Before anyone could stop him, Bill was cartwheeling round the ring.

"Where are the leetle clown's parents, pleeze?" asked Frederico, looking hopefully into the audience.

But Bill's mum
was still in the
popcorn queue
and didn't have

the faintest idea of what was
going on.

"Leetle clown, stop now!"
insisted Frederico, but the Great
Bilbo wasn't going to stop for
anyone.

He was having the time of his
life! He grabbed a custard pie
and threw it in Frederico's face.

"*That's* how you do it!" he cried. The crowd clapped and cheered while Bill bowed and did a silly walk all round the ring.

"No, no! Come here now!" shouted the clown, wiping the foam from his eyes.

"You can't catch me! I'm the Great Bilbo!" sang Bill. He ran round the ring, picking up the clown's custard pies and throwing them in all directions.

"Don't use up all the pies!" cried Frederico. "We need them for our act!" But the Great Bilbo wasn't listening. The other clowns chased after him, but he dodged out of their way.

Splat! Spludge! Squelch! Large blobs of cream were flying everywhere. The crowd went wild, whooping and cheering.

It was the funniest clown show they had ever seen! Bill was so excited he decided to perform a front-flip – something he had never managed to do before, not even on the soft mats in P.E.

"Careful, not so fast!" warned
Frederico, but it was too late.
The Great Bilbo flung himself
forward, slipped on some foam,
tripped over the microphone
lead and landed on the sawdust
with a loud THUMP!

"Aaagh!" cried out Bill, in
pain.

The audience thought it was part of the act and screamed with laughter.

"It's NOT funny!" he shouted. "I've broken my leg!"

Frederico snapped his fingers. The lights went up, and the band stopped playing.

click

A First-Aider ran on to the stage, closely folowed by Bill's mum, who had

just walked down the steps with her box of popcorn.

One by one, the people in the crowd stopped laughing. There were murmurs and worried gasps as the Great Bilbo was carried out of the ring on a stretcher.

"Oh, Bill," Mum sighed. "What have you done now?"

Chapter Four

Bill sat miserably on a trunk
amid a pile of costumes while
they waited for the Circus
Doctor. The clowns finished their
act and ran straight past him,
moaning and complaining.

In the corner, a little
dog with a ruff
round his neck was
practising jumps through
a hoop. A juggler was throwing
clubs into the air and a man
walked past with an elephant.
Bill had always wanted to know
what it was like behind the
stage of a circus but, right now,
he just wanted to go home.

"You'd better get it checked at the hospital," said the Circus Doctor. "Don't worry, I don't think you've done any serious damage." But Bill had never felt so bad in his life.

A few minutes later, a tall man in a jogging suit came over. He had grey hair and glasses and was as thin as could be.

"Poor Bilbo," he said. "Does it hurt a lot?"

Bill nodded. "Who are you?" he asked, staring at the man's face.

"Don't you recognize me? I am Frederico, the clown!"

"You can't be!" replied Bill. "You're not speaking in that funny voice. And you're not wearing your costume."

"Being a clown is just my job,"
replied Frederico, whose real name
was Fred. "I would look silly if I
wore my costume in the street."

"Yes," said Bill quietly. "I'm
sorry. Did I spoil your act?"

Frederico shrugged. "I was
more worried that you had hurt
yourself," he said. He bent down
and put his hand on Bill's
shoulder. "The circus is a

dangerous place," he added. "Everyone has to obey the rules, even the clowns. Of course we want to make people laugh, but remember – being funny is a serious business!" Then he smiled and gave Bill a leaflet.

Frederico's School of Clowning!
Summer Holiday Workshops
for Children!

"I could teach you how to be a great clown," he said.

"Oh please, Mum!" begged Bill. "Please can I go?"

Mum thought for a few seconds. "I don't think so, Bill," she said finally. "I've had enough of your clowning around. It just gets you into trouble." She took the leaflet and folded it away in her handbag.

The Great Bilbo said nothing, but the tears ran down his hot red cheeks.

Chapter Five

The hospital said Bill's leg wasn't broken, but his ankle was badly bruised. A nurse wrapped it in a long white bandage and he spent the rest of the weekend lying on the sofa.

On Monday morning, it was time for school again. Bill hobbled out of bed and went to put on his clown costume. Then he stopped. And he thought.

"Clowns belong in the circus, not the classroom," he said to himself, and put on his school uniform.

For the rest of the week, Bill seemed like a different boy. He put his hand up when he wanted to say

something, and stopped doing
silly walks and funny voices.
Miss Carter couldn't believe
the transformation.

"Don't you want to be a
clown any more?" she asked,
pressing a 'Well Done' sticker
onto his T-shirt.

"Of course I do!" replied Bill.
"I'm going to be the Greatest
Bilbo ever!"

Every day, Bill rushed home from school to practise. He put on his baggy trousers, yellow shirt, silly blue wig and his red plastic nose. He learnt all the jokes in his *Hundred Best Jokes Book*. And when his ankle was completely better, he even taught himself to do a front-flip into the sand-pit in his garden.

Bill tried his best to be good for the rest of the term, but it wasn't always easy. True, he *did* lead the shark attack in the swimming

lesson. It *was* him that put a plastic spider in Alice's pencil

case. And when Miss Carter asked the class to think of something, "really, really precious,"

he was the one who shouted out,
"Tomato Ketchup!" But when
Bill brought home his School
Report, it was so much better,
that Mum thought she'd been
sent somebody else's by mistake!

"A report like this deserves a
reward," she said.

So in the holidays, Mum took
the Great Bilbo to Frederico's
School of Clowning where he
was taught all the tricks –

and all the *rules* – of the circus.

He learnt thirty-two more jokes, eight new falling-over routines and six magic knots

with a piece of string. He discovered how to spin plastic plates on the end of wobbly sticks, and learnt to juggle with clubs. He was taught to shut his eyes when being hit with a custard pie and nearly managed to ride a unicycle!

In fact, Frederico declared that Bill was his star-pupil. And do you know why? Because the Great Bilbo was the best-behaved clown in the class!

THE END